Near the end of the day, Lucy's world came crashing down. It was just before last period, and she was on her way out to the demonstration. She ran into Susan and was about to tell her the exciting news about Brad when she realized that she couldn't—absolutely *couldn't*—tell her. Brad had asked her out for tomorrow after school. *But I've got Habitat for Humanity tomorrow after school!* she thought frantically.

Lucy mumbled something about being excited about the demonstration and hurried away. What was she going to do? She'd made a commitment to Habitat.

But what about beautiful Brad Landers?

# 7th Heaven™

## THE NEW ME

by Amanda Christie

Based on the hit TV series
created by Brenda Hampton

And based on the following episodes:

"Life Is Too Beautiful"
Written by Brenda Hampton

"Yak Sada" ("One Voice")
Written by Elizabeth Orange

"Forget Me Not"
Written by Sue Tenney

Random House 🏠 New York

www.randomhouse.com/kids

Library of Congress Catalog Card Number: 00-1339768
ISBN: 0-375-81161-3

Printed in the United States of America
September 2000
10 9 8 7 6 5 4 3 2 1

# CONTENTS

1. 5:30?     1

2. The Assignment     15

3. Alienation...     19

4. ...and Connection     32

5. Soccer Practice and Cooking Class     43

6. First-Period Protest     55

7. The Hammer     60

8. Beautiful Brad     72

9. Late for Dinner     83

10. Lucy Lies     90

11. Habitat for Brad Landers     102

# 7th Heaven™

## THE NEW ME

## CHAPTER ONE

# 5:30?

It was Monday morning, and the hall was crowded with kids walking, talking, and laughing. Lucy Camden smiled as she rummaged through her locker. She wasn't sure why, but she felt good about herself today, really good. She felt strong and sure, as if there was nothing in the world she couldn't do.

Lucy shrugged. It was a strange feeling, but a good one.

Down the hall Lucy saw Jennifer Lewis, Stephanie Cobb, and Jan Porter laughing with their boyfriends.

*The A list,* Lucy thought. She smiled as she shut her locker. Usually, she felt a little self-conscious around them, but not today. Today, nothing could stop her. Lucy hoisted her books and started down the hall.

It was a beautiful morning. The sun slanted down through the windows above the lockers and shone on Lucy's hair. Out of the corner of her eye, Lucy saw the A-list boys glance at her as she went by. *That's weird,* Lucy thought. *Why would they be looking at me?*

The girls noticed their boyfriends noticing Lucy. They turned and stared daggers at her, but Lucy just drifted by.

Now other people were looking at her, too. They were staring at her, as if they couldn't believe their eyes. Lucy just smiled and kept on going.

And then she saw him. He turned the corner at the end of the hall and started toward her—Brad Landers, the most popular boy in school. He was the star of the football team and a student body leader. And he was gorgeous. He met Lucy's eyes and smiled.

Lucy's heart leaped in her chest. She had sudden visions of her and Brad talking over burgers at the pool hall, holding hands at the movies, and then kissing good night.

Brad was only a few paces away, close enough that Lucy could lose herself in his dark eyes. He held out his hand and started to…sing?

"Do Lord, oh, do Lord, oh, do remember me!"

*Huh?* thought Lucy. *What's he doing?*

Brad took her hand. "Do Lord, oh, do Lord, oh, do remember me…"

Lucy glanced around self-consciously. Jennifer, Stephanie, and Jan had their hands over their mouths. They were all laughing!

Lucy looked back at Brad as he built up to the big finish: "Look away beyond the blue!"

Suddenly, Lucy woke with a start. She was in bed, in Matt's old attic room, which she and Mary now shared. She breathed a sigh of relief. *Just a dream,* she thought.

She looked over at Mary, who was sound asleep. *What time is it?* Lucy thought, picking up the clock. *5:30? It's only 5:30?*

From somewhere downstairs, Lucy again heard, "Do Lord, oh, do Lord, oh, do remember me. Look away beyond the blue!" She groaned and tossed the clock across the room.

In the bed next to her, Mary stirred. "What? What is it?" she mumbled.

"Dad again!" Lucy said.

Mary groaned and buried her head under her pillow. Lucy sighed and closed her eyes, trying to find her way back into the good part of her dream, where she was before she'd been so rudely interrupted.

Downstairs, Simon woke to find Happy snuffling at his face. Simon pushed Happy away, stretched, then slipped out of bed.

"Do Lord, oh, do Lord..."

Simon rolled his eyes. *Dad's singing again,* he thought. He walked next door to check on the twins. Because his dad was still recovering from his heart attack and Matt had moved out of the house, Simon felt it was up to him to look after everybody.

It was completely quiet in the twins' room. Surprised, Simon peeked into their cribs. Both Sam and David were asleep. *That's pretty weird,* he thought. But when he glanced at his watch, he got a big surprise.

*It's only 5:30!*

He knew his dad was happy to be alive, but enough was enough! Simon spun on his heel, marched back to his room, and got back into bed.

Down the hall, Ruthie sleepily wandered

into her parents' room and climbed into their bed. "He's singing again," Ruthie said. "He never used to sing."

Mrs. Camden was wide awake and staring at the ceiling. "Sure he did," she said.

"Not like this," said Ruthie.

Mrs. Camden sighed. "It's okay. Daddy's just really happy, and he wants to share his happiness...nighttime, daytime, all the time. Let's get under the covers and see if we can't sleep another minute or two."

Ruthie snuggled up next to her mom, and they firmly shut their eyes.

Downstairs in the kitchen, Rev. Camden was squeezing an orange and singing at the top of his lungs. "Look away beyond the blue!" Once the orange was spent, the reverend tossed the peel in the garbage, danced over to the phone, and dialed a number.

Across town, in a very small and messy apartment, the phone rang. Matt Camden and his roommate, John, both jumped out of their beds and began searching frantically through piles of clothes on the floor. Finally, Matt discovered the phone under a pizza box and yesterday's jeans.

"Hello!" he said. But the caller immediately hung up.

John staggered back to bed. "Man, when I find out who's been calling here every morning—"

"Don't look at me," Matt said. "I don't know who it is." He glanced at his watch.

*5:30!* he thought. *I'm going to be late for work!*

He quickly stuffed his legs into the pair of jeans he'd just grabbed from the floor, threw on a clean shirt, and rushed out the door.

"Hey!" John called after him. "We've got to clean this place up when you get home!"

Back in the Camdens' kitchen, Rev. Camden was chuckling as he tried to juggle the phone and a new orange.

Mrs. Camden came in carrying the twins. "Who could you possibly be calling at this hour?" she asked.

The reverend put down the phone and orange, gave his wife a big kiss, and took one of the twins from her.

"Our oldest son," he said.

"He shouldn't be home now," Mrs. Camden said as she put David into his high chair.

"He has a job, don't you remember?"

"Of course I do," said the reverend, putting Sam into his high chair. "And I want him to keep it. That was a wake-up call. I call every morning, just in case."

Mrs. Camden looked at him sternly. "You know you're supposed to stay off the phone. No calls equals no stress, remember?"

"I'm not stressed," Rev. Camden said, dancing around the kitchen again. "Life has given me a second chance, and I'm going to give life a second chance."

Mrs. Camden giggled as the reverend grabbed her and spun her around. In the doorway, Ruthie rolled her eyes. She'd followed her mom downstairs, but there was no way she was getting involved in this silliness.

She headed back toward the stairs and ran into Simon in the foyer. "I can't take all this happiness!" Ruthie said. "I want Dad to go back to normal so I can get some sleep."

Simon nodded sagely. "Eventually, things will go back to normal. But until then, I'm looking after things around here. Did you do your homework?"

Ruthie's jaw dropped open.

Simon continued, "I'd like to check your homework before you go to school. You know, like Dad would if he wasn't supposed to be resting."

Ruthie snapped her mouth shut. "I'm not showing you my homework!" she said. "I don't have to. I know if I did it or not."

Simon looked at her expectantly. "Well? Did you?" he asked.

Ruthie frowned. "I still have time," she said, hurrying up the stairs.

"I'm still going to want to see it!" Simon called after her. He shook his head. "Kids."

In the kitchen, Simon found his mom and dad feeding the twins. He clipped a newspaper article onto the refrigerator. "Just a little something for you to read when you get a moment," he said to his mom.

Mrs. Camden raised an eyebrow. "Thank you, Simon," she said. "When I get a moment, I will."

Simon put his hand on his dad's shoulder. "I'll finish up here," he said. "You should be meditating."

The reverend looked at his son with surprise. "Thank you, Simon, but I'll meditate later, when the house is quiet."

Simon shook his head. "The trick is to meditate now, when the house is noisy. That's the challenge. After all, how often is the house going to be quiet? And if noise is your excuse, then you won't ever do it, right?"

The reverend and Mrs. Camden looked at each other in surprise. "You know, I think that's right," the reverend said. "Thank you, Simon." Rev. Camden handed Simon Sam's spoon, gave Simon his seat, and headed upstairs.

"What's with the newspaper clipping?" Mrs. Camden asked.

"Oh, it's just an article someone from my home ec class gave me about cooking for people with heart disease," Simon said as he spooned baby food into Sam's mouth. "I thought you might be interested."

Hiding a smile behind her hand, Mrs. Camden said, "Thanks, Simon."

Upstairs in the attic room, Mary and Lucy were getting ready for school. Lucy lay on her bed and stared at the ceiling as she waited for Mary to finish in front of the mirror.

"I had the best dream this morning," Lucy said.

"Let me guess," said Mary, putting on lip-stick. "Boys."

Lucy looked at her sister. "Am I *that* obvi-ous?" she asked.

Mary grinned. "Pretty much," she said, puckering her lips at the mirror. "It's not like you think about much else."

Lucy gasped. "That's not true!"

Mary looked at her sister in the mirror and raised an eyebrow.

"Okay, so maybe it's true," Lucy said. "But that's perfectly normal. I'm a healthy teenage girl."

"Hey, don't look at me," Mary said. "I didn't say there was anything wrong with it. So what was the dream?"

Lucy sighed. "Brad Landers."

"Oh," Mary said. "Brad Landers, huh? How did he find his way into your dream?"

"I've been tutoring him in math," Lucy said guiltily.

"And you didn't tell me?" Mary said, pre-tending outrage. "So? How's it been?"

Lucy groaned. "Difficult," she said.

"I can imagine," Mary said.

Lucy nodded. "He's just so gorgeous that it's

hard to look at him. But then I catch myself staring! And he's really nice, too."

"I know," Mary said. "You wonder how anyone that good-looking could avoid being stuck up. It's almost unfair."

Lucy nodded.

"So…the dream?" Mary said.

"Oh, yeah," said Lucy. "It was weird. I think I was popular."

"Really?" Mary said.

"Uh-huh," said Lucy. "I was feeling really good about myself, like there was nothing I couldn't handle, you know?"

Mary nodded. "It's called 'confidence.'"

"And then the boys started staring at me and Brad walked up…Of course, Dad ruined it all with his singing."

Mary laughed. "Definitely a dream," she said. She paused for a moment, looking at her younger sister. "But you know, it doesn't have to be."

"What do you mean?" Lucy asked.

"You're so smart," Mary said. "All you need to do is focus on something other than boys. Figure yourself out a little bit.

"And it wouldn't hurt to wear a little

makeup," Mary continued. "Why don't you do something fancier with your hair? I think you'd be surprised at what could happen."

Lucy wrinkled her nose. "Who has the time? Besides, that stuff isn't important. If I ever do anything like that, I'll do it for my own reasons, not so people will like me. No offense."

"None taken," Mary said, blotting her lips with a tissue.

"If people can't like me as I am, then I don't want to know them."

"Right," Mary said. "Nobody's worth that kind of trouble."

They looked at each other. "Except Brad Landers," they said simultaneously.

They laughed, and Mary closed her lipstick case. "Let's get out of here," she said, picking up her bag.

"Did you get your math quiz signed yet?" Lucy asked.

"Oh, right," Mary said, putting down her bag. "I forgot. I'd better go find Dad."

"But we're not supposed to upset him. Why don't you ask Mom?" said Lucy.

"Because right now, Dad's un-upsettable."

"But still, should you take advantage of his…his…"

"His post–heart attack insanity?" Mary asked.

Lucy nodded.

"Definitely," Mary said. "Besides, Mom says it won't last long, so we might as well enjoy it while we can. Want to come?"

Lucy shrugged. "Why not? Even in his insanity, he's still Dad and you're still you. This should be interesting."

Lucy grabbed her bag and followed Mary downstairs to their parents' room. Inside, they found their father sitting cross-legged on the floor, with his hands resting on his knees. His eyes were closed.

Mary knocked lightly on the door. "Dad?"

The reverend smiled and, without opening his eyes, motioned for them to come in. "Mary and…Lucy, right?"

The girls looked at each other, impressed. "Pretty good, Dad," Lucy said.

The reverend grinned. "Would you two like to join me for a little early morning meditation?" he asked.

"Ah, no, that's okay," Mary said. "We've got

to get off to school. That's why I need you to sign this."

Mary handed over her test. The reverend opened his eyes and blinked at the paper a few times, trying to focus.

"What happened?" he asked when he saw the grade.

Mary shrugged. "I don't know," she said. "I did the homework the night before, but I had a hard time with it. The teacher didn't go over it before she busted us with this pop quiz."

The reverend motioned for Mary to join him on the floor. Mary looked pleadingly at Lucy, but Lucy smiled and slipped out the door, laughing as she headed downstairs to the kitchen.

*So much for post–heart attack insanity,* Lucy thought.

## CHAPTER TWO

# THE ASSIGNMENT

Lucy found Simon sitting at the kitchen table slurping up a bowl of cereal. Their mom was talking into the phone.

"Eric's fine, Mrs. Beeker," she was saying. She sounded exasperated. "He plans to be back the week after next. There's nothing for you to worry about...Yes, Mrs. Beeker, I'm busy, but I'll find a way to manage..."

Lucy sat down and reached for the cereal. "Mrs. Beeker again, huh?" she asked.

Simon nodded. "Did you do your homework?" he asked.

"Mind your own business," Lucy said, pouring cereal into a bowl.

"It *is* my business," Simon said.

Mrs. Camden hung up the phone and

walked over to the table. She looked tired and a little cross.

Simon said, "I'll round up the other kids as soon as I shave."

Lucy stared at her brother. "Shave?"

"Yeah," Simon said, as if Lucy were an idiot. "*Shave.*"

Mrs. Camden fought back a smile. "Simon, when did you start shaving?" she asked.

"When Dad came home from the hospital," Simon said. He got up, put his bowl in the sink, and headed upstairs.

Lucy and her mother exchanged an amused glance. "What's Mary doing?" Mrs. Camden asked, sitting down next to Lucy and resting her head on her hand.

"Dad cornered her about her math quiz."

Mrs. Camden frowned. "He doesn't need to be talking to anyone about a math quiz. He's supposed to be meditating. It's important for him to relax."

"I'm fine," said the reverend, walking into the kitchen with Mary. "In fact, I just had a great idea. It came to me while I was helping Mary with her math quiz. It's all about connection..."

The reverend clasped his hands together.

"And alienation," he finished, spreading his arms wide.

The three women watched his hands, then looked at each other with puzzled expressions. *What's he talking about now?* Lucy thought.

"You see," he continued, "when Mary came to me to sign this failed pop quiz, she was reaching out to me, and that sparked something. I realized that the way to reconnect with an alienated person is to ask for their help."

He paused, but no one responded.

"I think it would be a wonderful experience for the kids if each of them goes to school today and enlists the aid of someone whom they've previously alienated."

Mary and Lucy looked uneasy.

"I just know it'll be a wonderful experience for all of you," said the reverend. "Will you do it? For me?"

"Okay," Mary said.

"Sure, Dad," said Lucy.

"And will you ask Simon and Ruthie to do it, too?" the reverend asked.

Mary and Lucy nodded. *Oh, yeah,* Lucy thought. *If we have to do this, they definitely do.*

Just then, Matt burst through the back door. "I've got a fifteen-minute break," he said. "Can I take a shower?"

Before anyone could respond, he was vaulting up the steps.

"Him, too?" Mary asked, pointing to Matt.

"Yes," the reverend said. "Matt, too."

In the bathroom, Simon had covered his face with shaving cream and was peering into the mirror, razor poised for its first stroke, when Matt barged in.

"Hey, watch it!" Simon said.

"What are you doing?" Matt asked.

"What does it look like I'm doing?"

"It looks like you're about to shave," Matt said with a grin.

Simon glared at him. "So?" he asked.

"So, nothing," Matt said. He stripped off his clothes and stepped into the shower. From behind the curtain, Simon could hear his brother laughing.

Simon looked at himself in the mirror. "No crying," he said. "You're the man of the house now, so no crying!"

He took a deep breath and began shaving.

## CHAPTER THREE

# ALIENATION...

Lucy closed her locker and turned around. It was Monday morning, and the hall was full of kids walking, talking, and laughing. Just a few lockers down, Jennifer, Stephanie, Jan, and their boyfriends were hanging out.

Lucy smiled. It was just like her dream. *Except Brad Landers isn't going to come around the corner and make me the most popular girl in school,* she thought. *Or sing "Do Lord, oh, do Lord, oh, do remember me!"*

Lucy watched as Jan glanced at her, then looked quickly away. There was a time when she and Jan had been good friends. But then something had happened. Jan had become popular, and Lucy hadn't, so Jan suddenly stopped talking to her. And that was that.

At the time, Lucy had been really upset. But she'd gotten over it. And now she and Jan just pretended not to know each other.

"Hey, what are you doing?"

Lucy turned around to find her big sister standing next to her.

"Nothing," Lucy said. "Just thinking."

"How are you doing with Dad's project?" Mary asked. "Any luck connecting with some alienated people?"

Lucy looked at Jan again, but she was busy laughing at something Stephanie was saying.

"No," Lucy said. "I can't seem to find any." Although she knew a great candidate was staring her right in the face.

Mary laughed, then lowered her voice. "How about the junior class three stooges?"

Lucy looked across the hall and saw the girls Mary was talking about—Susan Gertz, Lisa Lunby, and Carol Overhill. They were dressed in overalls and had handkerchiefs tied over their hair, as if they were cleaning ladies.

"No way," Lucy said. "They're weird. *Too* weird. I don't want to go that far with Dad's wacky idea."

"Good," Mary said. "So here's how you can help me."

"Help *you?*" Lucy asked. "I don't think that's what Dad had in mind."

"I don't know," Mary said. "I do leave you out of my life all the time..." Mary spread her hands wide. "Alienation," she said, gesturing to the space between her hands. "So now I'm going to let you do something for me," she said as she clasped her hands together. "Connection!"

Lucy rolled her eyes.

Mary grinned. "Come on. Coach is going to be a half hour late for practice. Will you meet me after school in the gym and try to keep the ball away from me? I want to work on my defense."

"Uh-huh," Lucy said. "Why me?"

"Because you're shorter than a real player, so it's more of a challenge. Besides, I'm looking to get Dad's assignment over with, too."

"I see," Lucy said. "But I haven't felt the..." —Lucy spread her hands apart—"alienation, so I don't feel a need for the"—Lucy clasped her hands together— "connection."

Mary frowned. "Fine. You know what your problem is? You don't have anything like basketball. Next year, you're going to be a senior. You're going to be trying to figure out which college you want to go to and what you want to do with your life, and I hope no one helps you decide what you want to do."

Surprised at how upset Mary was, Lucy said, "Okay, okay, if it means that much to you—"

"Forget it," Mary said, cutting her off.

Stunned, Lucy watched her sister stomp off down the hall.

Simon thought his arms were going to break. He'd just visited the school's library and taken out every book he could find on heart attacks, diet, and exercise.

*Maybe I'm overdoing it,* he thought, peering over the stack of books in his arms. *If I can just get to my locker...*

Just then, Simon collided with something— or someone—much bigger than he was. The stack of books instantly crashed to the floor.

Simon glanced up and found himself look- ing at a mountain of a boy. Simon didn't know his name, but he knew he played on the foot-ball team. And he didn't look happy.

*Maybe if I confuse him by talking really fast, he won't kill me,* Simon thought. "Sorry," Simon said quickly, bending down to collect his books. "I couldn't see where I was going. See, I'm doing a little research on hereditary disease and cholesterol and heart attacks and stuff, since my dad just had a heart attack…"

Suddenly, Simon found the big kid kneeling beside him, helping him pick up the books.

"How far were you planning on juggling this stuff?" the big guy asked.

Simon stood up, balancing the stack in his arms again. "Just to my locker," he said.

The guy nodded. "Here, I'll take them."

Simon looked at him in surprise. "Really?"

"Uh-huh," the kid said, holding out his arms. Simon slid the stack over. "Thanks," Simon said.

"Don't mention it. My name's Jim, by the way," he said.

"Simon," said Simon. "I'm usually up to carrying a load of books, but now that I'm the man of the house, and I've got three sisters and six-month-old twins to take care of,

I've got to admit, I'm a little worn out.

"Not that I'm not up to the job," Simon emphasized. "It's just new to me, that's all."

"Your dad died?" Jim asked, looking completely shocked.

"No, no, he's fine," Simon said. "He's taking it easy for a few weeks, so I'm filling in."

"So he's going to be okay?" Jim asked.

Simon nodded. "It was just a mild heart attack. He has to change his diet and start exercising and stuff like that."

Jim frowned. "What are you, a wimp? You've got nothing to complain about," he said, dumping the books back into Simon's arms and walking off.

Simon watched him go. Totally confused, he staggered toward his locker.

Lucy spent the entire day thinking about what Mary had said that morning. As irritating as it was, Lucy knew she was right. She *didn't* know what she wanted to do with her life. In fact, she didn't have the slightest clue. It was scary, but maybe it was time to start thinking about some larger issues.

When she got home that night, Lucy went in search of the new man of the house.

Simon was up in Ruthie's room. His little sister was listening to her radio and bouncing around the room. *I guess this is what the kids are calling "dancing" these days,* Simon thought. He walked over to the radio and shut it off.

"Hey, what's the big idea?" Ruthie asked.

Simon put his hands on his hips. "*You* were supposed to take a bath."

Ruthie put her hands on her hips. "*I* did," she said.

Simon squinted his eyes at her. "If you did, then you didn't use a towel. I was just in the bathroom, and they're bone-dry."

"You know," Ruthie said, "you're really starting to get on my nerves."

"I wouldn't have to get on your nerves if you'd just do what you're supposed to," Simon said. "Now go take a bath."

"Fine," Ruthie said, flouncing toward the door.

"Wait!" Simon suddenly called.

Ruthie spun around. "Which is it, go or wait?" she asked.

Simon slowly turned. "Did you try to make friends with any alienated kids today?" he asked.

Ruthie blinked and then said, "I tried, but Ricky said his parents are American citizens."

*Huh?* Simon thought as Ruthie left. He was starting after her when Lucy appeared in the doorway.

"Hey," she said. "Do you have a second?"

"Me?" Simon asked.

"Yes, you," Lucy said. "I have a question, and I don't want to bother Dad."

"Really?" Simon said, pleased.

"Yes, really," Lucy said.

Down the hall, Simon heard the water come on in the bathroom. *Good, Ruthie's filling the tub,* he thought.

"Okay," Simon said, perching on the bed and crossing his arms. "Fire away."

"Well," said Lucy, leaning against the door-jamb, "I was talking to Mary today about Dad's project, and she ended up getting mad at me and accusing me of not knowing what I was doing with my life. I got to thinking about it, and I think she's right. So what I wanted to ask you was, do you have any idea what I should be when I grow up?"

Simon was shocked. He stared at Lucy, his mind a complete blank. *My first week as man of the house, and I get this kind of question?* he thought. But he knew his sister trusted him, so he had to think of something. Suddenly, Simon had an idea.

"Okay," Simon said. "In the past, what has made you feel the happiest and the most fulfilled?"

Lucy thought about it. Immediately, her exboyfriend Jordan came to mind—she remembered laughing with him, flirting, just spending time together. She sighed, a happy grin on her face. Simon cleared his throat and she glanced at him.

"Let me guess," he said. "Boys. You can't base your life on boys, you know."

Lucy scowled at him. "Gee, thanks. *I* could've told me that," she said, and whisked out of the room.

Simon sighed. *I guess being man of the house means sometimes saying things people don't want to hear,* he thought.

Just then, Matt poked his head through the doorway and pointed at Simon's face. "Hey, I think you've got a five o'clock shadow, pal."

Simon put his hand to his cheek. He'd heard that shaving made your beard grow in faster and darker. But his cheek felt as smooth as it always did.

Matt laughed. "Yeah, sure you do!" he said, walking down the hall.

Simon suddenly felt the sting of tears in his eyes, but he quickly fought them back. *No!* he thought. *No crying!*

Matt was still chuckling as he walked into the bathroom.

"Don't you ever knock?"

Matt looked over at the tub. Ruthie was lounging on the edge, her back against the wall and her feet propped up, reading a book.

"Sorry," he said. He was about to start collecting the things he needed for the evening when he noticed that the tub was full of hot water.

"What are you doing?" he asked his little sister.

"Simon told me to take a bath," Ruthie said.

"So then take a bath," said Matt.

"But I'm not dirty," Ruthie said.

"Then don't take a bath," Matt said.

"Really?" Ruthie said.

"Really," said Matt.

Ruthie jumped up and gave Matt a big kiss. "Thanks!" she said, and scampered out the door.

Matt shook his head. Had the whole house gone crazy since he'd left? He was opening the medicine cabinet when someone cleared her throat behind him. He turned to find Lucy standing in the doorway.

"Hey," he said.

"Hey," said Lucy. "Can I ask you something?"

Ruthie pranced down the hall to Simon's room and poked her head in the door.

"Matt said I don't have to take a bath!" she exclaimed. She stuck her tongue out at Simon and scurried away.

Simon jumped up from his desk and marched down the hall to the bathroom. Lucy was standing in the doorway, nodding her head. Simon could hear Matt saying, "Well, you're good at the stuff Mom's good at. You both have mechanical skills, and you like fixing cars and—"

Simon didn't wait for Matt to finish. He pushed past Lucy and saw his older brother sitting on the edge of the tub, which, Simon noted, was full of clean water. "Did you tell Ruthie she didn't have to take a bath?" he demanded.

"Yeah," Matt said, irritated at the interruption. "What's it to you?"

"It's my job, that's what," Simon said. He glared at Lucy. "And what's Lucy doing here?"

"I'm talking to him about my future, if that's okay with you," Lucy said.

"No, it's *not* okay!" Simon said.

"Well, that's too bad, Simon, because Matt might actually be helpful," Lucy said.

Simon gasped. Immediately, Lucy regretted her words, but before she could apologize, Simon had fled down the hall.

"What was that all about?" Matt asked.

Lucy shook her head. "I'm not sure," she said, looking after him.

"Well, anyway," Matt said, "I guess what I'm saying is that maybe you should go to technical school and be a mechanic. Something like that."

"A mechanic?" Lucy said. "I don't want to

be a mechanic. I want to do something important."

"Hey," Matt said. "You ever have the brakes
on the car go out on you?"

Lucy rolled her eyes.

"There are also lots of guys at mechanical
school," Matt said with a grin.

Lucy glared at Matt. "Guys? Why does
everyone think that's all I'm interested in!"

"Well, isn't it?" Matt asked.

Lucy groaned. "Thanks a lot," she said. She
headed for the attic stairs, feeling sick to her
stomach. *Is that all people see when they look at
me?* she thought. Lucy shook her head. *Simon
and Mary are right. I've got to think about something other than boys.*

Lucy paused for a moment, deep in
thought.

*Matt's right, too. I do love mechanical things,
like when Mary, Mom, and I fixed up that car for
Matt. I was good at it, too,* she thought.

*Come on, Lucy. What makes you feel the
happiest and the most fulfilled?* Suddenly, an
incredible idea came to her. She smiled and ran
up the attic steps. Maybe she had an answer!

## CHAPTER FOUR

# ... AND CONNECTION

That night, Lucy made a bunch of phone calls and spent hours doing research on the Web. When she got to school the next day, she knew what she had to do.

After getting her books and closing her locker, she turned to survey the scene. As usual, the hall was crowded and busy. As usual, Jennifer, Stephanie, and Jan were standing at Jan's locker with their boyfriends. And, as usual, standing right across the hall were the three stooges of Lucy's class, Carol Overhill, Lisa Lunby, and Susan Gertz. Just like yesterday, they were dressed in drab clothes. But today, Lucy actually knew why.

Lucy took a deep breath and walked over to

them. Susan saw her coming and froze in the middle of what she was saying.

"Hi," Lucy said.

"Hi," whispered Susan.

"Hi!" chirped Lisa with a too-big smile.

"Hi," Carol said stiffly.

"I'm Lucy Cam—"

"We know who you are," said Carol. "What do you want?"

Lucy paused. This was going to be harder than she'd thought. "I heard you guys are involved with Habitat for Humanity…?"

She waited, but the three girls just looked at her.

"I'd like to volunteer," Lucy said. "I thought maybe you could tell me a little about it."

"*You* want to volunteer for Habitat for Humanity?" Carol asked. "You know that you have to get your hands dirty there, don't you?"

"Of course," Lucy said. "You'll have to see it to believe it, but I'm actually pretty good with a hammer."

Carol snorted. "You're right. I don't believe that at all."

Susan suddenly spoke up. "What about

your...social schedule?" she asked shyly. "Are you sure you have time?"

"Yeah," Carol said. "Habitat requires real commitment. You can't just show up when you feel like it."

"I know," Lucy said. "I'm thinking of making this the kind of work that I do for the rest of my life. So I'm pretty serious about it."

Carol looked very skeptical, but Susan said quietly, "We *do* need more people."

"And it would be great to get someone off the B list," Lisa gushed.

"B list?" Lucy said.

"Well, you're not on the A list," said Carol.

"No, of course not," Lucy said. "I had no idea I was even on the B list."

Carol looked Lucy over carefully. "If you're doing it to meet guys, forget it. Most of them are older and married."

Lucy felt herself turn red. Did *everyone* know about her and boys?

"I'm not doing it to meet guys," Lucy said.

"Right," Carol said. "Well, if you're still interested at the end of the day, meet us in the lobby. Let's go, girls."

Lisa and Susan followed Carol down the

hall. "Bye!" Lisa said cheerily. Susan just waved. Lucy watched them go.

*B list?* she thought. She suddenly felt a glow of pleasure come over her. *Wow, not bad!*

Just then, Lucy heard quiet laughter from across the hall. Their boyfriends were gone, but Jennifer, Stephanie, and Jan were still there, watching her. As Jennifer and Stephanie turned to go, Jan said something to them. They rolled their eyes and continued down the hall without her. Jan crossed the hall toward Lucy.

"Hi," she said.

"Hi," Lucy replied.

Jan looked around quickly, then said, "Want some advice?"

"Sure," Lucy said.

"You were very close to being on the A list when you went out with Jordan last year. Did you know that?"

"No," Lucy said.

Jan nodded. "Anyway, I'd just hate to see you blow it." Jan glanced around again and then started to walk away.

"Jan, wait," Lucy said. "I appreciate the advice. I appreciate you talking to me, with my being on the *B list* and all. But I have to tell you, those women are doing something so cool that blowing my chances at the A list just doesn't measure up."

Jan shrugged and continued on down the hall. Lucy turned and walked the other way.

Simon hadn't had a good day. He'd spent all of school feeling bad about what Matt and Lucy had said to him the night before. And he even felt bad about feeling bad. He figured that the man of the house wasn't supposed to get his feelings hurt. He was supposed to suck it up and move on.

As he left the school that afternoon, he wondered if it could get any worse.

"How's the man-of-the-house job coming along?" he heard from behind him.

Simon turned to see Jim catching up to him.

Simon turned and kept walking. "Okay, I guess," he said.

"Hey, Simon," Jim said.

Simon looked up at him. Jim was staring at Simon's face. "You've got a little something…" he said, pointing to his chin.

Simon automatically reached up and found

a piece of toilet paper stuck to his face. *Oh, no!* Simon thought. He'd cut himself shaving that morning and had stuck the little piece of toilet paper there to stop the bleeding. He'd forgotten all about it, and it had been hanging on his chin ever since!

Angrily, Simon wiped it off. "Nobody ever tells you these things," he said.

"Don't worry about it," Jim said, giving Simon a smile. "Men do that all the time."

"Really?" Simon asked.

"Oh, yeah," said Jim. "Happened to me when I first started shaving."

Simon sighed. "To tell you the truth, I'm turning out to be pretty bad at this whole man-of-the-house thing. No one's really paying attention to me."

"And it hurts your feelings, doesn't it?" Jim said.

"No, it's not that," Simon said.

"Makes you want to cry?" Jim asked.

"No," Simon said. "It doesn't make me want to cry." But even Jim's just mentioning it made him want to.

Jim didn't seem to notice. "When my dad died," he said, "I didn't think I could cry. I

mean, men aren't supposed to cry, right? But
then one night I started, and I couldn't stop. My
mom totally freaked. She made me take up
football so I wouldn't turn out to be some sort
of sissy. But I used to come home from practice
crying, so then she got me in this boys' group
where I had this fake dad coming around trying to influence me. I still couldn't quit crying."

"What happened?" Simon asked.

"We both went to see your dad," Jim said.
"And he told me that I can cry and still be a
man, and I can also get my feelings hurt and
still be a man, because men have feelings, too.
Then I didn't feel so much like crying all the
time, just once in a while. And now I let that
fake-dad guy stick around."

Jim grinned. "And as it turns out, I love
football."

Simon smiled.

"Well, I've got practice," Jim said. "I just
wanted to see how things were going. I felt
pretty bad calling you a wimp and all yesterday.
Sorry about that."

"Don't worry about it," said Simon.

"Tell your dad hello for me," Jim said. "And
get him to teach you how to shave."

"I will," Simon said. "Thanks."

"Don't mention it," Jim said. A couple of guys passed by on their way to the football field. "Come on, Weepy!" they said. "We've got practice!"

Jim turned back to Simon. "Weepy's my nickname." He shrugged and smiled. "What do I care?" He waved and jogged toward the field.

Simon smiled and headed for the parking lot. But his smile disappeared when he saw Matt waiting to pick him up. Immediately, all Simon's confused feelings from the night before resurfaced.

Ruthie was in the backseat.

"Where's Mom?" Simon asked.

"Busy," Matt said. "And Mary's got practice. Get in and let's get out of here."

"What about Lucy?"

"I dropped off Mom's toolbox to her at school. She's off on some big secret adventure."

"And what is the big secret adventure?" Simon asked.

Matt shrugged. "It probably involves boys."

"Probably," Ruthie chimed in from the back.

"You should have found out," Simon said.

Matt looked at Simon. "Why, little man? What difference does it make?"

"Okay, that's it!" Simon said. "Get out of the car!"

"Oh, boy," Ruthie said. "Brother against brother. I haven't seen this since the Civil War."

Simon frowned at Ruthie, then quickly turned back to Matt. "You heard me. Get out!"

Matt laughed. "Why? Are you planning on beating me up?"

"No, I'm planning on telling you off. So get out and take it like a man."

Ruthie unbuckled her seat belt. "If there's going to be a fight, I'd like to jump in like a woman," she said.

"Stay in the car," Simon commanded. He watched as Matt opened his door, slid out, and walked around the front of the car.

"Okay, Simon," Matt said. "What's this all about?"

"You know what this is all about," Simon said. "You moved out and left me to take care of Mom and Dad and the kids."

"I didn't leave you to take care of anyone," Matt said.

"Yeah? Well, nevertheless I *am* taking care of everyone, and you are undermining my authority."

Matt crossed his arms. "How?" he asked.

"By telling Ruthie she doesn't have to take a bath," Simon said. "And...and...all kinds of stuff."

"What kinds of stuff?" Matt asked.

*The shaving!* Simon wanted to say, but he felt tears welling up behind his eyes. No matter what Jim had just told him, he didn't want to cry in front of Matt.

"Just stuff, okay?" he said.

"Don't get so upset," Matt said.

"It's too late!" Simon said. "I am upset. You act like this is all so funny, like I'm some kind of idiot or something."

"When did I ever act like you were an idiot?" Matt asked, shocked.

Now Simon had to say it. "When I was shaving," he said quietly. "And it hurt my feelings. Did anyone laugh at you when *you* first started shaving?"

Simon couldn't help himself now. He sniffled and wiped at his face as tears slid down his cheeks.

Matt looked stunned. "Simon, I'm sorry," he finally said.

"It's okay," he replied. "I just wanted you to know."

"It's not okay," Matt said. "I feel terrible."

"No, really," Simon said. "It's fine."

Matt gave Simon a hug, which made Simon cry harder. Matt looked down at his younger brother and couldn't help getting teary-eyed himself.

"I'm sorry," Matt said again as they got into the car.

"Me too," said Simon.

"It's been a tough couple of weeks," Matt said.

In the backseat, Ruthie just shook her head. "When are things going to go back to normal?" she asked.

## CHAPTER FIVE

# SOCCER PRACTICE AND COOKING CLASS

Lucy met Carol, Lisa, and Susan after school in the lobby, as they'd discussed. Carol was surprised to see her but wouldn't admit it. Lisa was overjoyed, and Susan just smiled quietly. The girls gave her some of their extra work clothes to change into—a T-shirt, sweatpants, and a sweatshirt. And, of course, a bandanna for her hair.

Lucy was nervous on the drive out. What if Habitat didn't live up to her expectations? What if it turned out *not* to be what she wanted to do with the rest of her life?

Lucy sighed. *Nothing ventured, nothing gained,* she thought. *If this isn't it, I'll just keep looking. Now that I've started, it won't be so hard to keep going.*

\* \* \*

Around seven o'clock that night, Lucy's new friends dropped her off at her house. She waved good-bye and staggered through the kitchen door. She was exhausted and dirty, but she'd never been happier in her life. There was no doubt left in her mind. Habitat was great!

She'd crossed the kitchen and opened the refrigerator door before she realized that Mary was sitting at the kitchen table with their neighbor, Mrs. Beeker.

"Uh, hi," Lucy said. "What's going on?"

"Mrs. Beeker's helping me with my math homework," Mary said.

Lucy just stared at the two of them. Mrs. Beeker was a big gossip and was always nosing around, especially since the reverend's heart attack. Lucy couldn't imagine what she was doing in the house.

But there she sat. "I left you a plate in the microwave," she said to Lucy. "And dessert's in the fridge."

"Lemon meringue," Mary said.

Lucy looked in the fridge. "Oh, yeah," she said.

"I'm going to go check on the twins," Mrs.

Beeker said, getting up. "And then I'd better be taking off."

"Okay," Lucy said, watching her go. She looked back at Mary. "What's she doing here?"

"Helping out Mom," Mary said. "I know, who would have guessed? But she's actually helped me out, too. Someone's finally explained trigonometry to me in a way that makes sense."

Lucy nodded dully.

Mary cocked an eyebrow at her. "So are you going to get something out of the fridge or are you trying to cool down the entire house?"

"Whoops!" Lucy said. She grabbed a bottle of cold water and drained half of it down.

"Whoa!" Mary said. "So what did you do with your new weird friends that involves dirt?"

Lucy closed the fridge and went to the sink to refill the bottle. "How did you—"

"I saw you getting all buddy-buddy with them in the hall this afternoon," Mary said. "You realize that hanging with the three stooges is social suicide, don't you?"

"Don't call them that," Lucy said. "And I don't care about social suicide."

She put the bottle back in the fridge and collapsed in the chair next to Mary's. "I've got much larger things to think about now."

"Like?" Mary asked.

"Like the rest of my life. I think I've decided what I'm going to do with it," Lucy said.

Mary waited. "Uh-huh..."

Lucy smiled helplessly at her sister. "I joined Habitat for Humanity," she said. "It is *so* cool. Mom let me borrow her tools, and this guy showed me how to put shingles on a roof, and I roofed!"

"So there *is* a guy involved," Mary said.

"Yeah, he's seventy!" Lucy said. "He's a master carpenter, and he helped me and my new friends roof an entire house—a house that people are going to live in, people who never had a house before. It's perfect. I get to do something I love—building and working with tools—and at the same time, help people in need."

"And you can work for Habitat for Humanity for the rest of your life?" Mary asked.

"I hope so," Lucy said. "I'd like to design and build low-income housing and volunteer whatever time I have while I'm learning to do that."

Mary sat back and looked at her sister admiringly. "Wow. This is unbelievable. I'm really, really proud of you."

"Thanks, but I owe it all to you," Lucy said. "If you hadn't started me thinking about all of this, I wouldn't have done it."

Mary grinned. As they hugged, Mrs. Beeker passed through on her way out. "I just love this family!" she said.

Mary and Lucy looked at each other and laughed.

Upstairs, Simon knocked on Ruthie's door.

"Come in!" she called.

Simon opened the door to find Ruthie sitting on the floor, coloring. Ruthie looked up. When she saw who it was, she said, "Get out."

Simon sighed. "I'm not here to bug you about your homework. I'm sure you're doing your homework, even though that's a coloring book you have there. I just wanted to ask if you've had an opportunity to make any new friends at school yet."

"Yes, I made a new friend," Ruthie said. "So get off my back."

"Who is it?" Simon asked.

"My teacher," said Ruthie. "I asked her to help me with the homework, and she practically did it for me. That's why I have time to color."

Simon raised an eyebrow.

"What?" Ruthie said. "I did a good thing. All the kids hate her, and now I don't. I think she's great. And if she keeps helping me like she did today, I could become an artist."

She held up her book and showed Simon what she was working on.

"Wonderful," Simon said.

"Want to join me?" Ruthie asked.

"I don't think so," he replied.

"Too *girly* for you?" she teased.

Simon smiled. "Yeah," he said, and closed the door behind him.

The next morning at breakfast, Lucy told her mom and Ruthie all about Habitat for Humanity and her life's plan.

"I've always wanted to work with Habitat," Mrs. Camden said. "They do great things."

"I was hoping you could teach me some practical skills," Lucy said. "So I could contribute more."

"Sure," said Mrs. Camden. "I'd be happy to teach my daughters anything I know."

"Which doesn't include trigonometry," Mary said with a smile.

"No," said Mrs. Camden. "Thank goodness we have Mrs. Beeker for that." She turned to Ruthie. "Speaking of homework, do you have yours done?"

"I finished it at school," Ruthie said.

"Good for you," said her mom. "But don't ask your teacher to do it for you again."

Upstairs in the bathroom, the Camden men were shaving. Rev. Camden, Matt, and Simon were squeezed in front of the same mirror, while the twins looked on.

"You missed a little something under your lip," Simon said to Matt.

"Very funny," Matt said.

"That was funny," said the reverend. "Simon's a funny guy, and a smart guy."

"And an excellent crier," said Matt.

Rev. Camden looked at Simon, concerned.

"You've been crying?" he asked.

"We both have," Matt said.

"It was no big deal," Simon explained. "Matt hurt my feelings, and I called him on it. We cried, we laughed, and then we made up."

"Oh," said the reverend. He smiled. "Good for you guys."

"Yeah," Matt said. "It wasn't too bad."

Simon grinned. Maybe things were looking up for him as the man of the house after all.

After they were finished in the bathroom, the men joined the women at the breakfast table. Lucy filled them in on her Habitat news and was roundly congratulated.

"What's your schedule like?" asked the reverend.

"I can go as often as I like," Lucy said. "They're in the middle of a big project and really need people, so I've committed to going after school three nights a week. If it's okay with you guys."

"Of course it's okay with us," said Mrs. Camden. "But that's a pretty busy schedule."

"I know," Lucy said. "But believe me, it's what I want."

Rev. Camden smiled. "Okay, but remember,

you're still young to have already decided what you want to do with the rest of your life. I know that right now this seems like the answer. And for right now, maybe it is. But that doesn't mean that it always has to be. Keep yourself open to new things and new opportunities, okay?"

Lucy smiled. "Thanks, Dad."

Rev. Camden gave her a hug. "I'm very proud of you," he said.

"Not to break up this lovefest or anything," said Matt. "But I've got to run to the exciting job that I definitely will *not* be doing for the rest of my life." He stuck a piece of toast in his mouth, grabbed his coat, and hurried out the door.

The reverend went upstairs to meditate. Everyone was getting up from the table when Simon clinked his glass with a spoon. "Excuse me! Can I have your attention, please? I've thought a lot about it, and I'd like a note so I can drop the home ec class I signed up for this semester."

Mrs. Camden started to say something, but Simon continued. "As man of the house, I've come to realize that men can cry and still be men. But men cannot cook. I just can't get the hang of it. I don't have the genes."

"Simon, that's ridiculous," Mrs. Camden said. "Some of the best cooks in the world are men. You're not dropping home ec. The point of the class is to get the hang of it."

"Mom, the class is just an elective," Simon said.

"So 'elect' to get the hang of it," Mrs. Camden said. "Besides, you have been bossing your sisters around for two days now, and I'm worried that you think you have more authority than them because you're a boy."

Simon started to say something, but his mother continued.

"*Parents* have the authority, Simon, a shared authority. And you, as an older sibling to Ruthie and the twins, have a responsibility to look after them and to have concern for all the members of your family. It's got nothing to do with being a boy."

Ruthie raised her hand.

"Yes?" her mother said.

"Did you remember that today's my day for snacks at…soccer practice?" Ruthie asked.

"No, I didn't remember," Mrs. Camden said. "I'm sorry, Ruthie."

"That's okay," Ruthie said. "I didn't remember to ask you until now."

"I can drop something off at school before practice is over," Mrs. Camden said. She looked in the freezer. "Would fish sticks be okay?"

"Are you kidding?" Ruthie asked. "For fish sticks, the team will make me king."

Mary rolled her eyes. "Oh, please," she said. "I can do better than that." She opened up a bag of cookies, dumped them in a plastic bag, and handed them to Ruthie. Ruthie gave her the thumbs-up.

As all the kids got ready to head to the car, Mrs. Camden pulled Mary aside to thank her. "And I was kidding about the fish sticks," she said.

"I figured," Mary replied. She hurried out of the kitchen and caught up with Ruthie.

"'The team will make me king?'" Mary said. "You almost blew it there, Your Majesty."

Lucy stopped at the door. "Blew what?" she asked.

"Nothing!" Ruthie said, sailing out the door.

Lucy looked at Simon. "Do you know what's going on with them?" she asked.

"No," Simon said. "And I don't care."

Lucy smirked. "They wouldn't tell you, would they?"

"Not even for money," Simon said. "But like I said, I don't care."

"You don't care because you have something of your own going on, don't you?" Lucy said.

"Just my life," Simon said. "And that's enough for me."

"You're lying," Lucy said. "You're doing that little squinty thing with your eyes."

Simon opened his eyes wide. "I don't know what you're talking about," he said, and scooted out the door.

"Why doesn't anyone ever tell me anything?" Lucy wondered aloud. But she didn't have time to worry about it just now. She had her own secret. Habitat for Humanity had opened Lucy's mind, and a whole new world awaited her. Come first period, she didn't intend to be at school.

## CHAPTER SIX

# FIRST-PERIOD PROTEST

"So what if you're better than the other girls?" Deena asked.

Simon cringed. He and his girlfriend were walking to their first-period class together—home ec.

"*Other* girls?" Simon asked. "Are you saying I'm a girl?"

"You know what I mean," Deena said.

"Yeah, I know exactly what you mean," Simon said. "You talked me into signing up for home ec so we could have a class together. But it never occurred to me that I'd be the only guy in the class."

Deena gave him a look. "It didn't?" she asked.

"Okay," Simon admitted. "Maybe it *did*

occur to me, and I didn't exactly *mind* the idea. After all, I'm getting in touch with my female side, and...well...you know."

"Uh-huh," Deena said.

"But I never thought I'd be so good at cooking that the girls would treat me as one of them...one of you...you know what I mean! It's hard enough being a guy and crying, let alone being a guy and cooking!"

Deena laughed. "Listen," she said. "If it bugs you that much, transfer out to wood shop."

"I can't transfer without a note," Simon said. "My mom already said no, and my dad will just say the same thing. Besides, I told them I was only doing this to flex my culinary muscles."

"They probably knew you were lying, so you should just be straight with them now. Tell them you'd rather be in wood shop because there are more guys there."

"And wood!" Simon pointed out. "Men love wood, you know? The smell of wood, the look of wood. The way it looks when it's varnished. The way it crackles in a fire. The way it can be as flexible as a piece of kite paper or as solid as the oak hull of a mighty Viking ship!"

Deena rolled her eyes.

"Wood," Simon said. "It's the substance of our lives."

Deena stared at him. "You're a total freak."

Now that she'd started helping people at Habitat for Humanity, Lucy found that she didn't want to stop. So when she saw a flyer announcing a demonstration for the rights of women in Afghanistan, she knew she had to go.

Lucy had study hall during first period. The principal had given her approval, and Lucy had joined the line of demonstrators holding signs and passing out leaflets to people driving by. At one point, Lucy saw her mother and hid her face behind her sign.

*Why did I do that?* she wondered. She had the principal's permission to be there, and she knew it was the right thing to do. She could *feel* that it was the right thing to do.

She ran into Carol, Lisa, and Susan in the hall right before second period and told them what she'd been up to.

"That is so cool!" Lisa said.

Carol nodded. "Very nice, Camden. Maybe

you've got what it takes after all."

Susan smiled shyly. "I've got a free period later today," she said. "I think I'll see if I can go, too."

"That's a great idea!" Lisa said.

"Thanks, guys," Lucy said. "It felt really great to be there. I owe it all to you and Habitat."

"You coming tomorrow?" Carol asked.

"Wouldn't miss it!" Lucy said.

The three girls said good-bye and headed on down the hall. Lucy turned and opened her locker. She was hurrying to get her books together for her morning classes when she heard laughter. She looked over and saw Jennifer, Stephanie, and Jan staring at her.

"Nice friends, Camden," Jennifer said.

"I guess it's the four stooges now," said Stephanie.

"Yeah, where's your bandanna?" asked Jennifer. The girls laughed as they drifted down the hall. This time, Jan joined in, too.

Lucy felt tears spring to her eyes. *They're not worth it*, she told herself. Still, she remembered what Jan had said yesterday...*You almost made the A list...*

Lucy shook her head, irritated at herself. She knew better. After all, what was the A list compared to what she'd just been doing on the picket line and what she did at Habitat last night? Absolutely nothing.

So how come it didn't feel that way?

## CHAPTER SEVEN

# THE HAMMER

Lucy did the best she could to bury the morning's bad feelings. But every time she passed Jennifer or Stephanie or one of their friends, they would point her out and laugh. Mercifully, Jan just pretended not to see her.

By the time she got home, Lucy was feeling completely drained. Mary passed her as Lucy climbed the attic stairs to their room.

"Hey," Lucy said.

"Hey," said Mary, hurrying by. It wasn't until Lucy had reached the top of the stairs and lain down on her bed that she realized Mary was up to something. She could just tell by the look on Mary's face.

*Ruthie!* Lucy thought. She bounded out of

bed and clattered down the stairs. She ran into her mother in the kitchen.

"Did Mary leave?" Lucy gasped.

"What's wrong?" Mrs. Camden asked.

"Nothing," Lucy said, struggling to regain her composure. "I just wanted to go with Mary to pick up Ruthie, that's all."

Mrs. Camden gave her daughter a look. "Why?" she asked suspiciously.

Lucy peered over her mother's shoulder. "Mom, if I don't leave now I'm going to miss Mary."

"You already have," Mrs. Camden said. They both listened as the car pulled out of the driveway and headed down the street.

Lucy's shoulders sagged. She turned to go back upstairs.

"You didn't answer my question," Mrs. Camden said.

Lucy turned around. "Huh?" she asked, suddenly exhausted again.

"Why did you want to go with your sister so badly?"

"Oh," Lucy said. She shrugged. "No reason." She turned and headed for the stairs.

Mrs. Camden raised an eyebrow. "Yeah, right."

At the elementary school, Ruthie was hiding in the bushes. She was waiting for her ride, but first she needed to see who was driving the car. She was relieved when Mary pulled up at the curb and not her mom.

Ruthie jumped out and ran over to the window. "Do I look cool?" Ruthie asked.

Mary whistled. Ruthie was decked out in a fully padded football uniform!

"You look downright frosty!" Mary said. "But how'd you play?"

Ruthie started to take off her forearm pads. "I don't want to brag," she said. "But I have moves on the field that *I've* never seen."

Mary laughed. "Go leave your stuff in your locker and hurry back before Mom gets suspicious."

"I'll be right back," Ruthie said, and jogged off toward the locker room.

Mary shook her head. If their mother ever discovered that Ruthie was playing football and not soccer…

\* \* \*

As she lay on her bed, Lucy heard Mary and Ruthie come up the stairs, talking in low tones.

*What are they up to?* Lucy wondered, and then sighed. *This is so stupid! Why am I feeling bad? Just because some girls I don't even know decided they don't like me?*

Lucy thought about how good she'd felt last night after Habitat and this morning after the demonstration. She smiled. *Yeah, that's what I should think about. After all, this is who I am now.*

Lucy sat up in bed. She'd suddenly had the best idea.

It was about an hour later when Simon burst into the room. "Lucy, I need your help!" he said. "Lucy...?"

The room was a mess. Clothes were scattered all over the bed, and the bureau was littered with open makeup cases.

"Down here!" Lucy said.

The closet doors were wide open and Lucy was all the way inside on her hands and knees, rummaging around.

"What's up, man of the house?" she asked, without turning around.

Simon sighed and started pacing. "I've got a problem, and I need a female perspective," he said.

"Uh-huh," came Lucy's muffled reply.

"You know this home ec class I've been trying to get out of?"

Lucy grunted.

"Well, the truth is, I only took the class to be with Deena, and now suddenly I'm one of the girls!"

From inside the closet, Lucy gave a cheer. She started to back out with a dress clutched in one hand.

"What are you so happy about?" Simon asked, slightly insulted.

"Oh, Simon," Lucy said, getting to her feet and hurrying to the bureau mirror. She held the dress up and scrutinized her reflection.

"That's just stupid," she said, turning around. "I spent last night—and will spend lots more nights—wearing overalls, carrying a hammer, and using a saw. But that doesn't make me a guy. How do you think this dress looks, by the way?"

Simon was staring at his sister, thunderstruck. She'd put up her hair and applied some very tasteful makeup. With the dress she was holding in front of herself, she was...

"Beautiful," Simon said.

"What?" Lucy asked.

"You're beautiful," Simon said. "When did you get so beautiful? I mean, you've always been beautiful. I never told you that because you're my sister, but now..."

"Really?" Lucy asked. She turned back to the mirror. "I was just playing around with a couple of new looks. I don't even know if I'm going to go with one of them full-time, if you know what I mean."

"Well," Simon said, "you should know that if you do, you're not making my job as your protector any easier."

Lucy turned and smiled. "Thank you, Simon."

The phone rang, and Simon picked it up. Lucy put down the dress and started looking through the closet again.

"Hello?" Simon said. "This is Simon... yeah...oh. Cinnamon. It's definitely cinnamon...no problem." He hung up and groaned. "You see?"

"What?" Lucy said.

"That was one of the home ec girls. She wasn't sure what she was missing from her snickerdoodles."

"How did you know it was cinnamon?" Lucy asked.

Simon put his head in his hands. "Because I just do!" he said. "I can't explain it. Haven't you been listening?"

Just then there was a tap at the door. It was Rev. Camden. "I'll listen. I'm a good listener," he said.

Simon sighed and stood up. "Never mind, it's nothing," he said. He slipped past his dad and hurried down the steps.

"What was that all about?" Rev. Camden asked. He sat down on Mary's bed and got his first look at Lucy. He suddenly found that he couldn't talk.

When she saw her father's reaction, Lucy laughed. "I tried a new makeover thing, okay?"

"Okay, sure," the reverend said. "Sure, I get it. It's, it's…you're beautiful."

"Thank you," Lucy said.

Rev. Camden coughed. "So anyway, I heard Habitat for Humanity bought that old place on Riverview Drive."

"Yeah," Lucy said. "The girls told me about it today. Apparently, the place looks worse than it is. The cornerstone and retaining walls are in good shape. There are a lot of dead walls that we'll have to modify, and we'll have to put new coping on all the exterior walls. You know, the ones that are masonry. But that's not so bad."

Rev. Camden nodded, as if he knew what Lucy was talking about. "No, that's not so bad at all. What's a little coping?"

Lucy smiled. "How are you doing, Dad?"

"It's been great having some time off," said the reverend.

"You haven't been on vacation, Dad. You had a heart attack," she said.

"Why split hairs?" the reverend said, smiling. "I couldn't be better. Well, if I knew what was going on with Simon, I probably could be better."

Lucy shook her head. "Not really," she said. "It's totally stupid."

Just then, Mary clattered up the steps. She stopped in her tracks when she caught sight of Lucy.

Rev. Camden glanced at Mary and stood up.

"Let me know if it gets less stupid, okay?" he asked.

Lucy nodded. The reverend gave Mary a kiss and headed downstairs. Lucy turned to Mary.

"So what's the deal with Ruthie?" Lucy asked.

"So what's the deal with *you*?" asked Mary.

"I tried something new, okay?" Lucy said.

"Sure," said Mary. "But why? What's going on?"

Lucy sighed and told Mary all about how Jennifer, Stephanie, and Jan had been acting toward her since she'd befriended Carol, Lisa, and Susan.

"I was afraid of that," Mary said.

Lucy nodded. "So I was sitting up here feeling sorry for myself when I remembered how good I'd felt just this morning and last night. It seemed stupid to stop feeling that way.

"At Habitat, I've started to see how the appearance of a house reflects on the people inside. I feel really good about myself right now, and I want my outside to reflect that. That way, if I start to feel bad again, I can look at myself in the mirror and remember the good feeling. Does that sound totally crazy?"

Mary grinned. "Not at all. And you look great. I told you, just a little makeup and a little something with your hair, and those A listers will be shaking in their boots."

"Thanks," Lucy said. "But that isn't the point."

"I know," Mary said. "The point is the way you're feeling on the inside. And that's what's really making the difference. I swear, you're positively glowing."

"Thanks again, but don't think I'm forgetting what I asked you," Lucy said. "So…?"

Mary glanced down the steps. Seeing no one, she walked over and sat down on her bed. "Ruthie's playing football, not soccer."

Lucy's eyes got big. "You're kidding!" she said. "Good for Ruthie."

"Yeah, well, it won't be so good if Mom finds out," Mary said. "If she discovers that her baby's nickname is the Hammer, she'll pull her right out. And that would really be too bad, because Ruthie likes it a lot. And she's *good*."

Lucy was flipping through dresses in the closet. "So how long do you and the Hammer think you can keep this little secret?"

"We just have to make it to the first game," Mary said. "Once Mom and Dad see Ruthie in all her gridiron glory, they'll have to let her do it. She has the swiveling-est hips you've ever seen. She can't be tackled. And if someone tries, it's Hammer time!"

Lucy laughed. "That's great."

"I know," Mary said. "But you can't say anything to Ruthie. I promised her I wouldn't say anything to anyone."

Lucy zipped her mouth shut.

Downstairs, Simon was coming out of the bathroom when he ran into his mom.

"If I might have a moment of your time?" Simon asked.

Mrs. Camden nodded.

"The thing is, this home ec class isn't turning out like I thought it would," Simon began. "You see, I—"

His mother sighed. "So you want to drop it because it's harder than you thought it'd be? Is that it? Because let me let you in on a little secret—life is often harder than you think it's going to be."

His mother continued on down the hall and went into her room. Simon sighed. "Yeah, especially *my* life."

He shook his head and went back to his room.

## CHAPTER EIGHT

# BEAUTIFUL BRAD

The next morning, Mrs. Camden waited to drop Ruthie off last. As Ruthie got out of the car, Mrs. Camden called to her, "Remember, mouth guard in, chin strap tight, and tuck the ball close to your body. Carrying it around like a loaf of bread is asking for a fumble."

Ruthie did a double take. "Huh?" she asked.

Mrs. Camden smiled. "You're playing football, not soccer, right?" she asked.

Ruthie put her hands on her hips. "Who blabbed?" she asked.

"No one," her mother said. She pulled a folded piece of paper out of her pocket and handed it to Ruthie. "You left this in your sweats."

On the paper was a list of Ruthie's equipment, including such items as shoulder pads and chin strap.

Ruthie groaned. "Are you going to make me quit?" she asked.

Mrs. Camden smiled and shook her head. "But I don't want you to tell Mary that I know."

Ruthie smiled back at her mother. "That's a good one, Mom," she said. "I promise."

"Just be careful!" she called as she pulled away.

Simon was explaining the intricacies of the snickerdoodle to his cooking partner when he saw his mom waving to him from the classroom door.

He glanced around—no one seemed to have noticed. "Excuse me," he said to his partner, and hurried to the door.

His mother was waiting for him in the hall. "Nice apron," she said with a grin.

Simon glanced down at the oversized white apron everyone in class had to wear. "What are you doing here?" he asked.

Mrs. Camden turned serious. "I felt like I brushed you off last night when you tried to talk to me about changing classes, so I stopped in to talk with your guidance counselor this morning. Evidently, you're a little more of a kitchen magician than you led me to believe. You want to tell me what's really going on?"

Simon blushed. "I'm sorry, Mom," he said. "I should have been straight with you. I only took the class so I could be with Deena. But as it turns out, I'm some kind of super chef, and everyone treats me like I'm one of the girls. I know there are a lot of great chefs who are men, but right now, it's just too much for me. I'd really rather be in wood shop."

Mrs. Camden nodded. "Well, there is your love of wood to consider," she said.

Simon grinned. "I just can't help it!" he said. "From paper to particle board and everything in between."

"Oh, I know," Mrs. Camden said. "I've got a thing for wood myself. Your counselor says you can transfer in."

"That's great," Simon said.

"Of course," said his mother. "Your first project in wood shop has to be a spice rack."

Simon grinned. "Thanks," he said.

"Don't mention it," she replied, opening her arms for a hug. Simon recoiled.

"What are you trying to do to me?" he asked, looking around.

"Oops," Mrs. Camden said. "Sorry! See you later."

Simon waved good-bye and slipped back into class.

After class Simon met Deena at the door.

"Is it just me," he said. "Or does the world seem different, as if the air itself is full of possibilities? Possibilities carefully crafted with wood?"

Deena smiled. "I assume that was your mother at the door?"

When Simon nodded, Deena said, "Congratulations. I knew your parents would be on your side if you just leveled with them. I hope you'll be very happy with your wood."

"Thank you," Simon said. "And I will. I love the smell of sawdust in the morning."

"So I guess that means I can have your snickerdoodle recipe?" Deena said.

"What?" Simon said. "Oh, I don't know..."

"What do you mean, you don't know? What do you need a snickerdoodle recipe for in wood shop?"

Simon shrugged. "I can't let that recipe fall into the wrong hands."

Deena glanced down at her hands. "What's wrong with these hands?"

Simon laughed as they headed down the hall to their next classes.

Lucy shut her locker and turned around. As usual, the hall was crowded with kids talking, laughing, and walking to class. As usual, Jennifer, Stephanie, and Jan stood with their boyfriends just a few lockers down. And, as usual, Lucy's new friends Carol, Lisa, and Susan were across the hall.

But, today, at least one thing was different—and that was Lucy. Not only did she feel different, she looked different. Today was the first day she was trying out her new look in school.

It wasn't a complicated look. She hadn't spent a lot of time in front of the mirror or anything. Like the night before, she'd applied a little makeup and put her hair up. And she was wearing a new, sleek dress. She felt great. For the first time in her life, she felt like she really knew who she was. And it came from the inside, not the outside.

And just like she'd always heard, it was as soon as you weren't concerned anymore that the outside responded. Stephanie, Jennifer, and Jan's boyfriends had noticed her. In fact, they couldn't seem to take their eyes off her.

Jennifer and Stephanie were furious. They were hissing insistently at their boyfriends, who muttered back in low tones. Only Jan seemed unmoved. Lucy couldn't read the expression on her face. Was it surprise? Maybe even…admiration?

Whatever it was, it didn't matter. There was no doubt about it—Lucy felt good, and she was determined to let herself enjoy the feeling. She was becoming someone, and it had nothing to do with Jennifer, Stephanie, Jan, *or* their boyfriends.

Lucy glided across the hall to say hello to her friends.

"Wow," Susan said. "You look beautiful!"

"Did you see the A listers checking you out?" Lisa said excitedly. "That's so cool!"

Lucy grinned and nodded. "It *is* really

something, isn't it?" The three of them laughed together.

"I don't know what you're all so excited about," Carol said. "Sure, Lucy, you look great. But don't forget, we get dirty at the end of the day."

"Oh, that reminds me," Lucy said. "I have study hall last period today, and I wanted to go to the demonstration again. Do you guys want to meet me there after school?"

Susan nodded. "I'm in," she said.

"Me too," said Lisa.

Carol looked bored. "Okay," she said. "But don't forget, Habitat's our first priority. See you guys later," she said, and started down the hall.

Lucy, Lisa, and Susan watched her go.

"Don't mind her," Susan said. "I think she's just a little jealous of you today. Carol would never admit it, but I think she's always secretly envied the A listers."

Lucy nodded. "Hasn't everybody?" she asked. "Well, I'll see you guys at the demonstration."

"See you!" her friends said. Lucy didn't look, but as she walked down the hall, she could sense people watching her—not only

Jennifer and Stephanie and their boyfriends, but a bunch of others, too.

Lucy just smiled and enjoyed it. In a week's time, they'd all be used to her and she'd be back to being anonymous. *So much the better,* she thought.

But suddenly Brad Landers turned the corner.

Lucy saw him before he saw her. He was just as stunning as ever, with his dark hair and dark eyes. He smiled and laughed as he walked down the hall, joking with friends as he went.

And then he saw her. His face instantly lit up, and he gave her a big smile. Brad and Lucy saw each other every few days or so in study hall, whenever he needed help with math. For some reason, it seemed like his smile today was brighter than usual. He was walking toward her purposefully. It was just like in her dream!

Lucy felt her legs get weak. *Don't be silly,* she thought.

"Hey," she said to him.

"Hey," Brad said. "You look *amazing* today."

"Thanks," Lucy said.

"May I walk you to your class?" Brad asked.

"There's something I've been wanting to ask you."

Lucy was sure she was going to pass out right there in the middle of the hallway. *Get a grip,* she ordered herself. *He probably has a question about his math homework.*

"Sure," she said, continuing on down the hall. Brad walked next to her. "So do you have it with you?" Lucy asked.

"Huh?" Brad asked.

"Your math homework," Lucy said.

"Oh, no," Brad said, smiling. "That's not it at all. I mean, it's sort of about that. What I mean is...well...you've helped me so much in math class. You've seen my tests and how much better I'm doing."

Lucy nodded. Brad was staring at the floor, thinking hard. Lucy suddenly realized he was nervous!

"I wondered if you'd like to get a burger with me after school tomorrow," he said. "I'd like to thank you for all the help you've given me."

He looked up at her with the most serious, sincere expression. Lucy felt as if she was melting.

"Of course, Brad," she heard herself saying, as if from a great distance. "That would be wonderful."

Immediately, his grin was back. "Great!" he said. "Great."

Like magic, they were standing at the door to Lucy's next class.

"So I'll talk to you tomorrow?" Brad asked. "Meet me in the parking lot. I've got a car and can drive us to the pool hall. Okay?"

Lucy nodded. She couldn't speak. The butterflies were swirling madly in her stomach.

"Okay, so I'll see you," Brad said.

Then the bell rang and he was gone.

Lucy floated through the rest of the day. People called out to her, complimented her on her new look, and she nodded in return, as if looking down on everything from a great height.

Near the end of the day, however, she came crashing down. It was just before last period, and Lucy was on her way out to the demonstration. She ran into Susan and was about to tell her the exciting news about Brad when she realized that she couldn't—absolutely couldn't—tell her. Brad had asked her out for tomorrow after school. *I've got Habitat for Humanity tomorrow after school!* she thought frantically.

Lucy mumbled something about being excited about the demonstration and hurried away. What was she going to do? She'd made a commitment to Habitat.

But what about beautiful Brad Landers?

## CHAPTER NINE

# LATE FOR DINNER

Lucy got to the demonstration and picked up a sign. Deep in thought, she joined the line of people protesting the treatment of women in Afghanistan. She was so out of it that she didn't even see her mom coming until she was standing right in front of her.

"It's my free period," Lucy tried to explain. "The principal said she was sure you'd approve."

Mrs. Camden smiled. "I know. She called me. And not only do I approve, I'm very proud of you."

Mrs. Camden gave Lucy a hug. Then she picked up a sign and joined the line. "I'd better call your dad and tell him we'll be a little late," she said, getting out her cell phone.

* * *

Matt and Simon were just coming in when the
phone rang. Rev. Camden was in the living
room with the twins. He picked up the phone
and listened for a moment. Then he said,
"Don't worry about a thing. We Camden men
can take care of ourselves."

He hung up and looked at the twins. "That
was your ma-ma," he said. "Can you say 'Ma-
ma'?"

The twins just looked at him.

Simon laughed. "I guess it's still too early
for that," he said.

"I guess so," said the reverend. "Okay, the
girls are going to be late, so it's up to us to get
things started. Matt, you're on bathroom duty.
I'll start a load of towels in the washer. And
Simon the Great can take over in the kitchen."

"Do you want snickerdoodles, brownies, or
chocolate chip cookies?" Simon asked.
"Personally, I'd go with the snickerdoodles.
They're lighter, so you can eat more."

Rev. Camden and Matt looked blankly at
Simon.

"What?" Simon said. "You thought I could
cook, like, a real dinner?"

Rev. Camden and Matt nodded.

Simon laughed and started toward the kitchen. "It's junior high home ec, not Marcella Hazan's cooking school."

Matt looked at his dad. "Marcella *Who's* cooking school?"

The reverend raised his hands helplessly. "I don't know."

Matt headed up the stairs. Rev. Camden looked at the twins. "Simon's going to cook," he said. "Can you say 'uh-oh'?"

Ruthie was waiting for her ride. She had another surprise.

Mary pulled up, took one look at Ruthie, and panicked. Ruthie had been socked in the right eye—and it had turned black-and-blue.

Mary jumped out of the car and ran over to Ruthie. "Ice pack!" Mary said. "We need an ice pack!"

Ruthie held up an ice pack.

"Are you okay?" Mary asked.

Ruthie snorted. "You should see the other guy," she said. "Don't worry, I'll live."

"But if Mom and Dad see you, I won't," Mary said.

"Can't help you there," Ruthie said. "That's your department."

Mary put the ice pack on Ruthie's eye and led her to the car. On the way home, they passed the demonstration.

"Look!" Ruthie said. "There's Mom and Lucy!"

Mary sighed. She figured if she was going to get it, she might as well get it now. She pulled over, and she and Ruthie got out.

"Hi, gang," Mrs. Camden said. Then she saw Ruthie's black eye.

"Look what I got playing soccer," Ruthie said to her mom, winking.

Mary saw the wink and did a double take. After looking at her mom, she realized that she already knew about Ruthie playing football. Mary shot a look at Lucy.

"Hey, don't look at me," Lucy said.

"Are you okay?" Mrs. Camden asked Ruthie.

Ruthie shrugged. "Things happen when you get tackled and there's a pileup—you don't want to know. But I couldn't be better."

Mrs. Camden looked at Mary. "You can't

hide anything from me," she said. "I'm the mom."

"Are you going to make her stop playing?" Mary asked.

"I already asked her," Ruthie said. "And she said no."

"So you knew that she knew?" Mary said.

"Yeah," replied Ruthie. "Good one, huh?" Ruthie then looked around at the demonstration. "So what are we doing here?"

Mrs. Camden smiled. "We'll take a break and explain it to you."

Just then, Carol, Lisa, and Susan walked up. "Hey," they said to Lucy.

"Oh, hey," Lucy said. "Is it time to go?"

The girls nodded. Lucy introduced them to the Camden women, then the four of them headed back to school to catch their ride to the Habitat house.

Lucy's second night at Habitat was just as great as the first. She forgot all about her problem as she concentrated on the job at hand. When she got home, she felt the sort of exhaustion that only hard work offers.

In the kitchen, Lucy found Mary making herself a sandwich.

"Hey," Mary said. "How'd it go tonight?"

"Great," Lucy said. "Well, sort of great."

Mary looked at her. "What's up?"

Lucy sighed and sat down at the table. "Brad Landers wants to take me out for burgers after school tomorrow to thank me for all the help I've given him in math."

Mary walked over to the table. "You're kidding me," she said.

Lucy shook her head.

"Wow," Mary said. "There's the B list, there's the A list, and then there's—"

"Brad Landers," Lucy finished.

Mary studied her sister for a moment. "Okay, so why aren't you screaming or something?"

"Because I'm supposed to install toilets at the Habitat house tomorrow."

Mary pulled out a chair and sat down next to Lucy. "Let me get this straight," she said. "Installing toilets or a date with Brad Landers? *There's* a no-brainer."

"But I just can't cancel on Habitat for a date with a guy...can I?"

Mary raised her eyebrows. "They only have to know you're canceling for a guy if you tell them you're canceling for a guy..."

Mary gave Lucy a look, then went back to her sandwich. Lucy got a drink and then dragged herself upstairs.

What was she going to do?

## CHAPTER TEN

# LUCY LIES

Lucy woke up the next morning still not sure. All through breakfast and all the way to school, she dreaded seeing her friends—she knew she'd need a decision by then.

Sure enough, when Lucy shut her locker and turned around, there they were.

*The three stooges,* Lucy thought, and then caught herself. *What am I thinking?*

"Hey!" Lisa said when Lucy walked over.

"I can't believe it's almost finished," Carol was saying.

"I know," said Susan. "A week ago it was a piece of land and a bunch of lumber, and now it's a house."

Lisa nodded. "Soon to be a home for someone who's never had one before."

Carol gave them a sly grin. "Habitat for Humanity is so cool," she said.

The three girls laughed. When Lucy didn't join in, Susan turned to her. "Are you okay?" she asked.

"Fine," Lucy said. Then, before she knew what she was doing, she blurted out, "I can't help after school today. Something's come up. A family thing. It's pretty serious. We're going away for the weekend to visit my grandfather— he isn't so well."

The three girls looked at her in shock. "Oh, my God, I'm so sorry," Lisa said.

"Yeah," Susan said. "Don't worry about Habitat. Family is family."

Carol nodded. "We'll all cover for you."

"You will?" Lucy said.

"Of course we will," Lisa said. "That's what friends are for."

Lucy struggled to smile. "I owe you guys," she said. "Thanks."

The girls nodded and gave her encouraging looks, then headed off down the hall.

Lucy stood there for a minute. At first she felt terrible. But her guilty feelings slowly faded. It was done and over with—and she was going out with Brad Landers!

Lucy had trouble focusing for the rest of the morning. She kept daydreaming about her and Brad at homecoming, her and Brad at the prom, and, despite herself, how Jennifer, Stephanie, and Jan would look as she and Brad became the most popular couple in school.

Lucy did her best to avoid Carol, Lisa, and Susan. When she did see them, she used sorrow as an excuse not to say very much. Her friends respected her silence. Lucy was surprised to find that she didn't even feel all that bad about deceiving them.

She ate lunch by herself, rather than have to talk to anyone and make up more stories about her afternoon. After lunch, Lucy tried to concentrate in class in the hopes that the end of the day would arrive more quickly. But despite her best efforts, the afternoon seemed twice as long.

Finally, the last bell rang. Lucy had to stop herself from running down the hall to her locker at full speed. She briskly collected her things from her locker and then went out to the parking lot. She had to look a little miserable, just in case one of her friends saw her. But she made it out of school without seeing anyone. From there, she was home free. The student parking lot was around the back of the school and Carol, Lisa, and Susan would be around front, waiting for their ride to the house.

For just a moment, Lucy felt a pang of regret that she wasn't going with them. But then she saw Brad. He was walking toward her, waving.

"Hey!" he said.

Even if she'd wanted to, Lucy couldn't have stopped the smile that spread across her face. "Hey!" she said. When he reached her, he touched her hand. There was a moment where Lucy was sure he would bend down and kiss her.

"Um," he said. "My car's right over here." He led her through the lines of cars filing out of the lot, calling to his friends, who seemed to be everyone in the entire school.

*I'm with Brad Landers,* Lucy thought. *Everyone is looking at me and wondering who I am. This is so great!*

Lucy briefly worried that word would get back to her friends that she'd left school with

Brad, but then she realized there was little chance of that. After all, who ever talked to the three stooges?

Brad escorted her to the side of a black Corvette.

"Wow," Lucy said. "Is this a sixty-eight?" she asked.

Brad nodded and opened the door for her. "Yeah," he said as Lucy sat down. He closed her door, then jogged around to his side and slid behind the wheel.

"I feel a little guilty about it," he continued. "I don't know anything about cars, but my dad loves them. He rebuilt this one from the ground up."

"It's beautiful," Lucy said.

"Yeah," said Brad. He turned the key and the engine roared to life. "Ready to go?" he asked.

Lucy nodded and settled back into her seat. She wasn't sure she'd ever felt so happy. Suddenly, she heard Simon's voice: *What makes you feel the happiest and the most fulfilled?*

Lucy shifted uncomfortably in her seat.

Once they got clear of the student parking lot, it was a quick drive to the pool hall. Brad parked and walked her inside. They settled into a table by the window.

"Lucy," Brad said. He looked at her and smiled. "I didn't ask you out just to thank you for your help—although that has been great. You're a great teacher, by the way."

"Thanks," Lucy said.

"I had an ulterior motive," Brad said.

Lucy raised her eyebrows. "And a good vocabulary," she said. She cringed. "Sorry. You were saying?"

Brad fiddled with his menu, then seemed to decide on something. He leaned forward. "Lucy, I've had a crush on you since the ninth grade. And every time I worked up enough courage to ask you out, you were always dating someone else."

For a moment, Lucy was stunned into silence. *Since the ninth grade?* Lucy thought.

"I mean," Brad was saying, "you're so beautiful and smart, and you seem to know who you are and what you want out of life. That's so rare…and so attractive."

"Really?" Lucy said.

Brad nodded. "Yeah," he said.

"Well," Lucy said, "I'm single now."

"I know," Brad replied.

Lucy felt faint. Her dream was coming true!

Brad leaned forward. "Lucy?" he said.

Lucy leaned forward, too. "Yes, Brad?" she asked.

Brad glanced over her shoulder and frowned.

"Do you know Susan Gertz from our school?"

Lucy nodded.

"Maybe that's why she and her friends have been staring at us since they came in," Brad said.

For a moment, Lucy couldn't move. Then slowly, she turned in her seat. Standing by the take-out counter were Carol, Lisa, and Susan.

She turned back to Brad. "Could you excuse me for just one second?" she asked.

Brad nodded. Lucy hopped off her chair and walked over to her friends.

"Hi," she said.

None of them said a word. Carol looked furious, Susan looked disappointed, and Lisa looked completely confused.

"This isn't what you think it is," Lucy said.

"I think we all know exactly what this is," Carol said.

"You blew off the project to have burgers with some guy?" Lisa asked, bewildered.

Susan opened her mouth. But then she just closed it and shook her head. The girls grabbed their food and quickly left.

Lucy walked back to the table, her head down.

"What was that all about?" Brad asked.

Lucy looked up and shook her head. "It's too much to go into," she said. "I'm sorry to do this, but would you mind taking me home? I need to think."

"Sure," Brad said. They left and got into Brad's car. Lucy didn't say a word the entire ride.

Brad dropped her off at her door once they arrived at the Camdens' house. "I'll call you," he said.

Lucy nodded and went inside. On her way upstairs, she ran into her father coming out of the twins' room.

"Hey, what are you doing here?" he asked. "No Habitat today?"

Lucy looked at him, then bowed her head and started to cry.

The reverend gave her a hug and patted her head. "Why so low?" he asked.

"Is there anything lower than low?" she responded, sniffling.

"The bottom?" Rev. Camden suggested.

"Well, then that's me," said Lucy.

Her father was quiet, waiting for an explanation.

Lucy sighed. "I kind of lied to my Habitat friends today so I could go out with this really cute guy, and then my friends saw me with the really cute guy. So now they know—"

"That you lied?" Rev. Camden finished. "Not 'kind of lied' but just plain old lied, right?"

Lucy nodded. After everything she'd discovered about herself, all those new and wonderful things, she'd been so ready to give it all up just for a boy.

"I feel like such a jerk," Lucy said. "And I'm really sorry I did it."

"Don't tell me," Rev. Camden said. "Tell your friends."

"They won't listen," Lucy said.

"If you apologize and they don't listen, then

it goes from being your problem to being theirs."

Lucy gave a feeble smile. "Thanks, Dad," she said.

Lucy went up to her room and buried herself in homework until dinner. She knew there was no use thinking about it now—Carol, Lisa, and Susan would be at Habitat until at least seven o'clock.

After dinner, Lucy came back upstairs and stared at the phone. She cringed as she thought about the way she'd acted, slinking around the school, avoiding her friends. If someone she knew had acted that way, she wouldn't have stood for it. And she couldn't believe the way she'd thought about her friends. *Did I really think of them as the Three Stooges?* she thought.

She sighed. Like her dad had just said, all she could do was try. She picked up the phone.

*Carol first,* she thought. *She'll be the hardest.*

Lucy dialed Carol's number and waited. Carol picked up and said hello.

"Carol, it's me," Lucy replied.

But that was as far as she got. Lucy heard a click, and then a dial tone. Suddenly, Lucy was afraid. What if her friends didn't let her apologize? What if they didn't even give her a chance? The whole future Lucy had imagined for herself—what she thought she wanted to do with her life—had she just bargained that all away? *How stupid could I be?* she thought.

Quickly, Lucy fumbled to dial Lisa's number. *Lisa will listen to me.*

But Lucy hadn't said three words before Lisa sobbed and said, "I hate you!" and hung up.

Now Lucy was starting to panic. *One last chance,* she thought as she dialed Susan's number. When Susan picked up, Lucy blurted out, "Susan, please don't hang up!"

There was a pause, then Lucy heard Susan say, "Okay."

Lucy breathed a quiet sigh of relief. "Thank you," she said. "Carol and Lisa wouldn't listen to me."

"That's because you lied to us," Susan said.

Lucy bit her lip. "I know," she said. "I'm *so* sorry. I made a huge mistake. I was afraid that if I said no to Brad, he might not ask me out again."

"Look, we all have other things in our lives," Susan said. "Boyfriends, jobs, schoolwork…

you have to prioritize. Decide what's important to you. No one's forcing you to be a part of Habitat."

Lucy tried to say something, but she just winced instead.

"If you're going to do it," Susan continued, "people are depending on you. So you have to *show up* when you're scheduled. If everyone canceled, where would we be?"

"What can I do to make up for today?" Lucy asked.

"Well...," Susan said. "We're going out to the house tomorrow afternoon, and we still need help with the plumbing."

"I'm there!" Lucy said.

"Don't say it unless you mean it, Lucy," Susan said.

"I mean it," she replied. "I will definitely be there. Thanks, Susan. Thanks for talking to me."

"Sure," Susan said. "We all make mistakes. I'll see you tomorrow."

Lucy hung up, a little relieved. But she couldn't relax yet. She had one more call to make. And this one would be the hardest of all.

## CHAPTER ELEVEN

# HABITAT FOR BRAD LANDERS

Slowly, Lucy dialed Brad's number.

"Hello?" Brad said.

"Brad, it's Lucy."

"Lucy!" Brad said. "Listen, I'm sorry about whatever happened today at the pool hall with your friends. But I still enjoyed hanging out with you."

Lucy smiled. "Me too," she said.

"Great!" Brad said. "Then come to the movies with me tomorrow afternoon."

Lucy closed her eyes and fell back on her bed. *Why does life have to be this hard?*

"I can't," she said. "If I say yes to you, I have to say no to something else, and I already did that once."

Brad was quiet for a moment. Then he said,

"Is this some other guy?"

Lucy laughed. "No, there's no other guy. Are you kidding? Brad, I...I really like you."

"Then I don't understand the problem," Brad said. He sounded hurt and confused.

Lucy took a deep breath. "Brad, I don't think I can see you anymore."

Brad was stunned. "Wow," he said. "We're not even going out yet, and you're already breaking up with me. Can you at least tell me why?"

"It's hard to explain," Lucy said. "It's got nothing to do with you. You..." Lucy closed her eyes and smiled. "You're perfect. It's me—I'm the one who's screwed up."

"That isn't true," Brad said.

"You know how you told me how attractive it is that I know who I am and what I want to do with my life?"

"Uh-huh," Brad said.

"Well, when I get around you, I kind of forget that. I forget who I am, and I do—and think—bad things about people I care about. And doing that is the old me, not the new me."

"Lucy," Brad said, "I just want to take you to the movies, not change your life."

Lucy smiled and shook her head. "You don't understand. It's like I'm Superman and you're kryptonite. Around you, I lose all my strength. And neither of us wants that."

There was a long, uncomfortable silence. "I'm sorry, Brad," Lucy finally said. "Maybe it'll be different someday. But for now, this is just the way it has to be."

They said good-bye, and Lucy hung up the phone.

It was one of the longest nights Lucy could remember. She felt awful. *It just isn't fair!* part of her screamed. But fair or not, she knew it was the *right* thing to do. It was the right thing for her and who she wanted to be.

The next day was a Saturday, so she let herself sleep late, ate a leisurely breakfast, and then changed for Habitat. When the doorbell rang, she ran down the steps.

"That's my ride," she called. "Bye, everybody!"

But when she opened the door, she found Brad Landers standing on the step. He was dressed in overalls, carrying a hammer—and grinning from ear to ear.

Despite herself, Lucy had to smile.

"Um…what are you doing?" she asked.

"Spending time with you any way I can," he answered. "After we got off the phone last night, I called Susan Gertz. I know all about what happened, and I'm sorry for putting you in that position. I don't ever want to do that to you again."

"Brad," Lucy said. "It wasn't—"

"Shhh," Brad said, cutting her off. "Susan said they could use another volunteer down at the house…"

For a moment, Lucy couldn't believe her ears. "You would do that for me?"

"I *am* doing that for you," Brad said.

Suddenly, Lucy felt like crying—she was so happy.

Brad leaned forward and lowered his voice. "There's only one problem," he said.

"What?" Lucy asked.

Brad glanced around and leaned in even closer. "You should know, I almost flunked out of shop."

They both laughed.

Brad held up the hammer in his hand. "So which end of this thing do I use again?"

Lucy smiled. "Just stick close to me."

Brad smiled back. "That's the plan."

Lucy couldn't stop smiling as Brad took her hand and they left the house to wait for their ride.

## MARY'S STORY

Big sis Mary seems to have it all together: She's practical, super-smart, beautiful, vivacious, and a rising star on her school's basketball team. But beneath her perfect exterior, sixteen-year-old Mary is struggling to figure out boys, friends, parents, and life in general—not to mention her younger sister Lucy!

*Available wherever books are sold!*
*ISBN: 0-375-80332-7*

# MATT'S STORY

As the oldest kid in the Camden clan and a college freshman, handsome eighteen-year-old Matt often bears the burden of playing referee between his siblings and his parents. Sometimes it's tough to balance family loyalty against a fierce desire for independence, but Matt has earned his reputation as the "responsible one"— *most* of the time.

*Available wherever books are sold!*
*ISBN: 0-375-80333-5*

RIVALS

For better or for worse, Mary and Lucy Camden have one thing in common: they're the oldest sisters in a *huge*, busy family! But sometimes the two of them hardly seem related: Strong, independent Mary hangs out on the basketball court, while sensitive, impulsive Lucy loves the mall. And when there's a cute guy involved, it's all-out war!

*Available wherever books are sold!*
*ISBN: 0-375-80337-8*

## MIDDLE SISTER

Sometimes being the middle girl in a big family is a tight squeeze—just ask Lucy Camden! It can be kind of tough when your older sister is a beautiful, popular basketball star and your adorable younger sister has a knack for getting her own way. Dealing with brothers isn't always easy, either. But Lucy is her own person and she's determined to stand out—no matter what!

*Available wherever books are sold!*
*ISBN: 0-375-80336-X*

# MR. NICE GUY

Simon Camden never gives up. When he wants something, he goes for it, no matter how much work (or begging!) it takes. Sometimes his brother and sisters get in the way, and often he feels as if his dog, Happy, is the only one who understands him. But despite his ambition, Simon is the first to help anyone in distress, even if it means putting some of his big plans on hold...

*Available wherever books are sold!*
*ISBN: 0-375-80338-6*

## SECRETS

Nothing but the truth…

Lucy's always the first to speak up—at home, at school, on student court. But now her words could ruin Mary's life. Will Lucy keep her secret, or will she finally speak out?

*Available wherever books are sold!*
*ISBN: 0-553-49359-0*

# THE PERFECT PLAN

Lucy and Mary are definitely up to something, but the rest of the family is so busy they don't seem to notice—except for sharp-eyed Simon, who's got a big surprise in store for his older sisters!

## SISTER TROUBLE

Sisters are sisters, no matter what. But things can change when everyone thinks that one Camden sister is an angel and the other is a total loser. Lucy's flying high with a new driver's license and an invitation to the party of the year. One problem—Mary's not on the guest list. But just because her sister is on the outs, should Lucy have to suffer for Mary's mistakes?

*Available wherever books are sold!*
*ISBN: 0-375-81158-3*